With love to all the children and staff at Aspire Nursery—and most of all to Vasilis. Thank you for the joy and inspiration.
JP

For Joe—I love you.
MPS

With thanks to Louise Jackson and Denise Johnstone-Burt

Text copyright © 2019 by Jane Porter
Illustrations copyright © 2019 by Maisie Paradise Shearring

First US edition 2021

Library of Congress Catalog Card Number pending
ISBN 978-1-5362-1123-8

20 21 22 23 24 25 CCP 10 9 8 7 6 5 4 3 2 1

Printed in Shenzhen, Guangdong, China

This book was typeset in Filosofia.
The illustrations were done in mixed media.

Candlewick Press
99 Dover Street
Somerville, Massachusetts 02144

www.candlewick.com

CANDLEWICK PRESS

THE BOY WHO LOVED EVERYONE

JANE PORTER   ILLUSTRATED BY MAISIE PARADISE SHEARRING

It was Dimitri's first day at his new preschool. He was very excited to be there.

At storytime, he rested his head on Liam's shoulder.

"I love you, Liam," he said with a sigh.

Liam didn't know what to say, so he said nothing.

Once all the children stopped wriggling,

the teacher began the story.

It was about a dragon, a volcano, and a magic teapot.

Dimitri thought it was an excellent story.

At outdoor time, Sophie, Stella, and Sue laughed and played together, like friends.

"I love you," Dimitri said, trailing after them.

The three friends blushed and giggled, then ran away.

So Dimitri visited the big tree on the playground.

Its leaves were shaped like hearts.

"I love you, tree," he said, and gave it a hug.

The tree didn't reply.

A line of ants marched by Dimitri.

"Hello, ants," said Dimitri. "I love you, too."

The ants just kept marching.

At lunchtime, Berthe served the kids lots of different foods. Dimitri was hungry, and everything tasted delicious.

"I love you, Berthe," said Dimitri.

"You mean you love my cooking!" said Berthe.

After lunch, Dimitri said
"I love you" to the guinea pig

and to the paintbrushes,
who didn't seem to mind.

He also said "I love you" to Big Andrew and Little Bea.

But whenever Dimitri said "I love you" to them or to any of the kids, they only joked or blushed or turned away.

When it was time to go home, Dimitri said goodbye to his teacher.

He also told her, "I love you."

"Dear Dimitri," she said. "I know you do. I'll see you again tomorrow, OK?"

Dimitri walked with his mother, past the bakery, through the park, and along the canal. On the way, they passed an old man sitting on a bench. He looked very tired.

"I love you, old man," said Dimitri.

"Who are you calling old?" snapped the man.

After that, Dimitri
grew very quiet.

At bedtime, Dimitri whispered,
"I love you, Mom."

"And I love you, Dimitri," she said.
"You're my best, best boy."

Dimitri smiled and sighed
and went to sleep.

The next morning, Dimitri told his mother that he didn't want to go back to preschool.

"Why not?" she asked.

"Because not one person there said that they love me."

Mom helped Dimitri put on his coat anyway and wrapped him up warm.

"People have lots of different ways of showing how they feel," she explained as they walked toward the canal.

"When you tell people you love them," she said, "even if they don't say it back or show it, they feel it. That's just the way love is. It can't help but spread and grow."

Dimitri and his mom passed the same old man sitting on the bench in the park. He had opened a can of tuna and was feeding it to the stray cats.

"You see?" said Mom. "That's his way of saying 'I love you' to those cats."

In the park, they saw Berthe on her way to Dimitri's

school, too. She gave them a big smile and a wave.

"Look," said Mom. "She's saying 'I love you' with her smile."

When Dimitri and his mom arrived
at preschool, Mom said goodbye
to Dimitri.

Beneath the big tree with heart-
shaped leaves, Dimitri saw Sophie,
Stella, and Sue feeding the birds.
He watched the tiny birds hop with
enjoyment, and he loved them right
away. Dimitri wanted to join in the
fun, but felt uncertain.

Then Stella saw him.

"Come and help us feed the birds, Dimitri," she said,
and the girls shared their packets of birdseed with him.
One bird even jumped onto Dimitri's hand and
tickled his palm with its lightness.

A warm feeling began to grow inside Dimitri.

A few moments later, Liam came over and gave Dimitri a kind hug.

"Hello, my friend! Will you sit by me at storytime again?" he asked.

The warm feeling in Dimitri grew bigger.

At storytime that morning, EVERYONE wanted to sit by Dimitri.

They made quite a pile. The pile made the teacher laugh.

"You funny children," she said. "I do love you!"

Then the teacher read them a story about a frog, a mountain, and a rabbit.

Dimitri loved it. Everyone loved it.

Even the guinea pig seemed to enjoy it.